D1054864

Delicious English
CARAMEL TREE

www.carameltree.com

How the Moon Is Made of Cheese

WITHDRAWN

Fitchburg Public Library
5530 Lacy Road
Fitchburg, WI 53711

CARAMEL TREE

Chapter 1

Edna

This is the story of how the moon is made of cheese. It is a true story. All you have to do to check if it is true is go to the moon.

Well, a long time ago, in the green fields of England, lived a milk cow named Edna. She liked to eat daisies and buttercups and grass. She chewed all her food fifteen times before swallowing it.

Edna was happy just being a milk cow. She spent the days quietly minding her own business. She ate, and chewed, and chewed, and chewed… (and chewed another eleven times) and then finally swallowed.

In the evenings, she delivered buckets full of fresh milk to the barn. She took extra care to walk to the barn as slowly and gently and calmly as possible. Slowly. Gently. Calmly. She wanted to deliver milk, not milkshake!

One day, while walking slowly and gently and calmly to the barn, Edna saw the strangest thing. She saw an elf's footprints.

Have you ever seen an elf's footprints? Well they look like this.

'Why is an elf walking in the sand?'
thought Edna. She knew that elves were
light and flew through the air. This elf had
to be in trouble.

Chapter 2
The Gift

As she looked around, she saw a tiny elf sitting by the wheelbarrow. He looked tired and drained.

"Oh dear," said Edna. "You look tired. Why don't you have a nice glass of milk? It will give you energy."

The elf was very pleased with Edna's kindness. He drank the delicious milk and felt stronger. His tiny wings flapped with new energy.

Do you drink milk when you are tired? You should. Milk gives you wings!

"Thank you," said the elf.

The little elf flew up above Edna's face.

Edna smiled. She wondered how it might feel to fly.

Then the elf said, "You are a kind cow. I will give you a special gift!"

A big flash of light made Edna close her eyes.

When Edna opened her eyes again, the elf was gone. *'Where is the gift?'* she thought. She could not see any gift.

"Moooo!" Edna screamed.

There were two huge, feathery wings sticking out from her back.

Edna flapped her new wings.

"Woooaaa!" she yelled as she rose into the air. "I think I am going to be sick!"

Edna was perfectly happy being slow, gentle, and calm. It kept her milk from going bad. Wings would definitely not be good for the milk.

Edna did not want the wings. "I must ask the little elf to take these wings away," she said.

Edna looked around, but the elf was gone. Edna tried to go after the tiny elf, but she could not find him.

Edna waited and waited, but the elf did not come back. Edna was stuck with the wings.

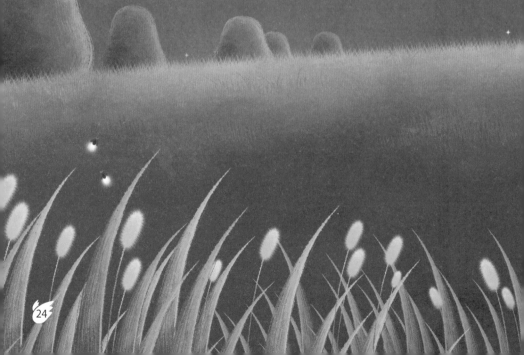

Chapter 4

Morris

Edna woke up the next morning to the sound of laughter. The other cows were laughing at Edna's wings.

"She thinks she can fly," teased one cow.

"Cows don't fly! Moomoo Heehee," laughed another cow.

Edna felt embarrassed. She couldn't hide her huge wings. She thought she might fly away, but she hated heights. So she just walked down to the field looking very sad.

As she walked, Edna saw her friend Morris, the field mouse.

"Oh, Morris," called Edna. "I am so embarrassed. I don't know what to do."

Morris was used to feeling embarrassed. Everyone thought he was strange because he insisted the moon was made of cheese. Morris loved cheese.

"Don't worry about them," he said. "You must prove to them that you can fly. I know you can." Morris tried to cheer Edna up.

Edna smiled. She thought about what Morris said and she agreed. She decided to prove to the other cows that she could fly.

"Are you ready to go for a ride?" Edna called.

Chapter 5

Look Up!

Morris jumped onto Edna's back and before he could say "giddy-up," Edna was flying.

Edna flapped her wings. Up and up they flew. Soon they were high above the fields.

"Yeeehaa!" shouted Morris. He was excited to be flying.

Edna looked down toward the other cows. The other cows looked up amazed and in shock. They were tiny specks in the field.

Suddenly, Edna's fear of heights struck her again. She was terrified of being so high up. Edna froze.

Edna and Morris began falling down to the ground like stones.

Morris quickly screamed, "Don't look down. Look up, look up. Yeeehaa!"

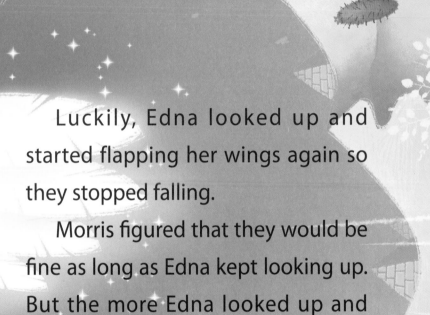

Luckily, Edna looked up and started flapping her wings again so they stopped falling.

Morris figured that they would be fine as long as Edna kept looking up. But the more Edna looked up and flapped her wings, the higher they went. At this rate, they would be on the moon by nighttime.

Chapter 6

Cheese

Edna had been flying for nearly three hours and it was getting dark. She was feeling very tired, but there was no way she could look down.

Edna and Morris flew higher and higher.
They were soon close to the moon.

"Great!" said Morris. "Now I can prove to
everyone that the moon is really made of
cheese."

Edna could see Morris getting more and more upset as they approached the moon. He could not see cheese anywhere. The moon was a silvery gray.

Edna did not like seeing Morris upset.

As soon as they landed on the moon, Edna started making cheese. She wanted to surprise her friend. All she needed was her

own milk, and with all the recent adventure, the milk was ready to become cheese.

Edna made so much cheese that it soon covered the moon.

And that's why everyone says that the moon is made of cheese. You can still see the cheese if you look through a telescope. Or you can e-mail an astronaut, she'll tell you.